My Weird School

Deck the Halls, We're Off the Walls!

Dan Gutman

Pictures by
Jim Paillot

SCHOLASTIC INC.

To my Facebook fans

ISBN 978-0-545-64012-1

Text copyright © 2013 by Dan Gutman. Illustrations copyright © 2013 by Jim Paillot.
All rights reserved. Published by Scholastic Inc., 557 Broadway, New York, NY 10012,
by arrangement with HarperCollins Children's Books, a division of
HarperCollins Publishers. SCHOLASTIC and associated logos are trademarks and/or
registered trademarks of Scholastic Inc.

12 11 10 9 8 7 6 5 4 3 2 1   14 15 16 17 18/0

Printed in the U.S.A.   40

First Scholastic printing, December 2013

Typography by Kate Engbring

Contents

The Best Christmas Vacation!

My name is A.J., and I hate it when a song gets stuck in my head.

Does that ever happen to you? You hear a song a couple of times and learn the words without even trying. Then you find yourself singing it *all* the time. You sing it while you're walking to school. You sing it while you're taking a bath. You can't stop singing it no matter where you are.

I *hate* when that happens!

Ever since Thanksgiving they've been playing this rap song on the radio over and over again. I can't get it out of my head.

The song is by this kid who isn't much older than me. His name is Johnny Cray, but his rap name is Cray-Z. My sister loves him. Every girl in the *world* loves him.

The song is called "The Christmas Klepto." It's about this mean guy who steals toys. It starts like this. . . .

'Twas the night before Christmas.
You know the rest.
Stuff was all over; the house was all messed.

I was dreaming of a Christmas white.
It was a totally silent night.

That's when I heard a crash and a boom,
So I ran right down to the living room.

There was this guy dressed all in black,
And over his shoulder he carried a sack.

I took one look at him and said, "Whoa, man!
I know you're not Frosty the Snowman."

"Who are you?" I asked after a pause.
"You sure don't look like Santa Claus."

He said, "The name's Klepto. I'm from
the South Pole.
I grab all your presents. That's how I roll.

"On Christmas Eve, I go around the world
and steal all the presents from boys and
girls."

Ugh. That song is the worst part about
Christmas. And now it's stuck in my head
forever.

Do you know what's the *best* part about Christmas? No school for nine whole days! That's right. No homework. No reading, writing, math, or social studies. No teachers.

Yippee!

Nine days! Do you know how long nine days is? I figured it out on my calculator. Nine days is the same as 216 hours. 216 hours is the same as 12,960 minutes. 12,960 minutes is the same as 777,600 seconds. That's a *long* time.

For 777,600 seconds I won't have to see Andrea Young, this annoying girl in my class with curly brown hair.

I'm going to enjoy every one of those seconds. This is going to be the greatest Christmas vacation of my life.

The First Rule of Being a Kid

I was eating breakfast when the greatest Christmas vacation of my life got even *greater.* My mom was sitting at the table reading her newspaper when I saw this on the back page. . . .

SANTA CLAUS IS COMING TO TOWN!

I leaned forward so I could read the
small letters. They said that Santa was
going to be at our local shopping mall on
Saturday, just before Christmas.

All my dreams had come true!

If you ask me, Santa Claus is the greatest

man in the history of the world. Anybody who gives toys to kids should get the No Bell Prize. But I figure Santa will never get the No Bell Prize, because that's a prize they give out to people who don't have bells. And if there's one thing Santa has plenty of, it's bells.

"Can you take me to the mall on Saturday?" I asked my mom. "Please, please, *please*?"

"Dad and I need to clean out the garage on Saturday," my mom replied.

"You can clean out the garage *anytime*, Mom," I told her. "Santa is only going to be at the mall on Saturday. If I don't go, I'll never get to see him for the rest of my *life*."

"Sorry, A.J. Not this Saturday."

"But I need to buy a present for Amy," I begged.

My sister, Amy, is three years older than me. She's annoying, but I have to get her a present anyway.

"No," Mom said. "No means *no*."

Hmmm. Begging usually works for me. I would have to try something else. If at first you don't succeed, try, try again. That's what my parents always say. You can accomplish *anything* if you put your mind to it.

It was time to put Plan B into effect.

I started crying.

If you want something really badly and

the situation is hopeless, there's only one thing to do—cry. That's the first rule of being a kid.

I peeked to see if my mom was watching me cry.

"A.J.," she said. "Those are crocodile tears."

What do crocodiles have to do with anything?

"Come on, Mom!" I pleaded. "I've been waiting to meet Santa Claus my whole life."

Mom put down her newspaper and looked at me. She had a serious look on her face.

"Your father and I have been meaning to tell you something for a while now, A.J.,"

she said. "It's about Santa Claus. We think it's time you knew that Santa—"

But she didn't get the chance to finish her sentence because the phone rang. I picked it up.

It was my friend Ryan, who will eat anything, even stuff that isn't food.

"Santa is coming to the mall!" Ryan

shouted into the phone.

"I know!" I shouted back. "Do you think it's the *real* Santa? I mean, how could he visit every mall in the world?"

"He's not visiting every mall in the world," Ryan told me. "He's just visiting *our* mall! That's why we have to be there. Are you in? My mom said she would drive us. Spread the word."

I hung up and called my friends Michael, Neil, and Alexia to tell them the big news about Santa.

"I want to go!" said Michael, who never ties his shoes.

"I want to go!" said Neil, who we call the nude kid even though he wears clothes.

"I want to go!" said Alexia, who rides a skateboard all the time.

In case you were wondering, everybody was saying they wanted to go.

I looked at my mom with my best puppy dog eyes. If you ever want something really badly, look at your parents with puppy dog eyes. That's the first rule of being a kid.

"Please?" I asked. "Ryan's mom said she'd drive us to the mall. You don't even have to go."

"You'll buy a present for your sister while you're there?" Mom asked.

"Of course!"

"Okay," my mom agreed. "You can go."

Yippee!

A Christmas Miracle

I had to wait a million hundred hours for Saturday to arrive. Wednesday felt like it was two days long. Thursday must have been three days long. Friday took at least a week. I thought I was gonna die of old age.

But finally, it was Saturday. My mom

14

made me wear the dorky red-and-green Christmas sweater that my aunt knitted for me last year. Ugh, it's itchy.

"Do I *have* to wear this?" I asked.

"Yes," my mom replied. "You want to look your best in front of Santa."

"I don't want to look like a dork in front of Santa," I said.

"You look very handsome, A.J."

When I came downstairs, my sister, Amy, was watching TV in the living room.

"Nice sweater, dork," she told me.

I didn't care what Amy said. It would be worth it to wear a dorky, itchy sweater if I could see Santa Claus live and in person.

I sat in the window for a million hundred minutes waiting for my ride. Finally, Ryan's minivan pulled up.* Ryan, Michael,

---

* I think it's called a minivan because it was invented by some lady named Minnie.

Neil, and Alexia were inside. They were all wearing their itchy Christmas sweaters.

"Nice sweaters, dorks," I said as I climbed in.

Lots of people had decorated their front yards for Christmas. We drove past

giant inflatable snowmen, candy canes, Santas, sleighs, and lots of reindeer. It was beautiful. Ryan's mom started to sing *"I'm dreaming of a white Christmas . . ."* and we all joined in.

That's when the most amazing thing in the history of the world happened.

It started to snow!

Well, that may not be all that amazing to *you*. But we live in California, and it hardly *ever* snows here.

"It's snowing!" we all marveled as we pressed our noses against the windows.

It was a Christmas miracle.

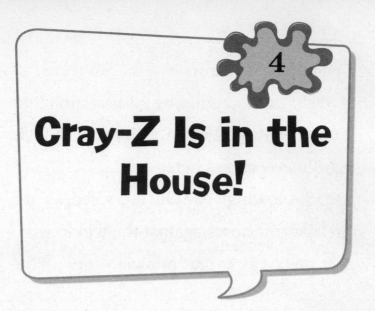

Cray-Z Is in the House!

When we got to the mall, the parking lot was jammed. Ryan's mom circled around trying to find a spot.

"Everybody must be here to see Santa," she said.

"I wonder where he parked his sleigh," Michael said, looking around.

"Santa doesn't park his sleigh in a parking lot, dumbhead," said Neil the nude kid. "That would be *crazy.*"

"Where do you think he parked it?" asked Alexia.

"Up on the roof, of course," said Neil.

Right next to the mall entrance was a big bus. On the side of bus, in big red letters, it said: CHRISTMAS RAPPIN' WITH CRAY-Z.

"Cray-Z is here!" shouted Alexia. "That must be his tour bus!"

"Cray-Z?" asked Ryan's mom. "Who's Cray-Z?"

Ryan's mom is really old, so she doesn't know anything. We had to tell her that

Cray-Z is this kid rapper, and his song "The Christmas Klepto" is on the radio all the time.

"Do you like his music?" Ryan's mom asked us.

"Ugh, no!" said Ryan.

"That kid is horrible," said Michael.

"I call him Justin Timberfake," said Neil.

We all said how much we couldn't stand Cray-Z's music. I didn't tell anyone that Cray-Z's dumb song had been stuck in my head all week.

Suddenly, a bunch of girls came running out of the mall. They surrounded the bus.

"We love Cray-Z!" they were shouting. "Marry me, Cray-Z!"

Those girls were screaming and crying

and fainting all over the place. What is their problem?

"Girls are weird," said Alexia, who is technically a girl but likes cool boy stuff anyway.

Finally, Ryan's mom found a parking spot. We had to walk a million hundred miles to get to the entrance of the mall.

"WOW!" we all said, which is "MOM" upside down.

When we walked through the door,

everything was *Christmas-y*. There were candy canes, wreaths, colored lights, jingle bells, and huge paper snowflakes all over the place. **MEET SANTA TODAY** said a banner on the wall. I could hear "Rudolph the Red Nosed Reindeer" playing. Big Christmas ornaments were hanging from the upper level of the mall. Zillions of people were walking around. There was electricity in the air!

Well, not really. If there was electricity in the air, we would get electrocuted.

"You're big kids now," Ryan's mom told us as she took a cell phone out of her pocketbook. "I'm going to do some Christmas shopping. We can stay in touch by phone."

She gave Ryan the cell phone and told him to put it in his pocket.

Cell phones are cool. My mom said I could get one when I'm in high school.

"We'll meet at the food court in two

hours," Ryan's mom told us. "I need you kids to stay together and be careful. Don't get into trouble, do you hear me?"

"*Us* get into trouble?" I asked.

"What could possibly happen?" asked Alexia.

"We *never* get into trouble," said Michael.

Ryan's mom looked at us with those crazy grown-up eyes that make it seem like she's drilling an invisible hole in your head. Then she left.

The mall is big. Right in the middle is a *ginormous* Christmas tree that almost reaches the ceiling. How they got that tree in the mall, I'll never know.

We walked all over the place looking for Santa.

"I'm glad Andrea and Emily aren't here," said Alexia. "They're so annoying."

"Hey, I have an idea," I said. "Let's use Ryan's cell phone and make a prank call to Andrea's house."

Everybody agreed that was a genius idea, so I should make the call. Ryan speed-dialed the number for Andrea's house.

"Hello?" somebody answered.

I wasn't sure if it was Andrea or her mother.

"I would like to order a large pepperoni pizza," I said.

"You must have the wrong number. This is not a pizza parlor."

The gang was cracking up. It was

definitely Andrea's mother on the phone.

"Do you have ravioli?" I asked.

"No!"

"How about spaghetti?"

"No!" Andrea's mother said. "Wait a minute. Is this A.J.? Are you calling for Andrea? She's not home. She's at the—"

I didn't hear the end of the sentence, because that's when the most amazing thing in the history of the world happened.

Somebody tapped me on the shoulder. But I'm not going to tell you who it was.

Okay, okay, I'll tell you. But you have to read the next chapter. So nah-nah-nah boo-boo on you.

True Love

5

"Hi Arlo!"

"Ahhhhhhhhhhhhhhh!"

It was Andrea! She's the only person in the world who calls me by my real name.*

I must have jumped three feet in the air. Little Miss Perfect was with her crybaby

* Because she knows I don't like it.

friend Emily. They were carrying a bunch of packages.

"What are *you* doing here?" I asked Andrea. "Buying yourself a new encyclopedia because your old one wore out?"

"Very funny," said Andrea. "Emily and I bought toys for homeless girls and boys."

"That's right," said Emily, who always agrees with everything Andrea says. "We want to bring peace and harmony to kids all over the world."

"Oh, yeah? Well, we came to meet Santa Claus," Alexia said.

"*Oooooo!*" Andrea said, all excited. "We want to meet Santa, *too*. Can we come with you guys?"

"We'll have to talk it over," I said.

The gang and I moved off to the side and huddled up like football players.

"What do you think?" asked Neil. "Should we let them hang out with us?"

"I say no," I said. "I don't want to walk around with Andrea all day."

"*Oooooo*, A.J. doesn't want to walk with

Andrea," said Ryan. "They must be in *love*!"

"Wait a minute!" I yelled. "I told you I *didn't* want to walk with Andrea. Why are you saying I'm in love with her?"

"A.J., everybody knows you love Andrea," said Neil. "It's totally obvious that you only said you didn't want to walk with her to hide the fact that you're in love with her."

Hmmmmm.

"Okay," I said, "in that case, it's okay with me if Andrea walks with us."

"*Oooooo*, A.J. wants to walk with Andrea!" said Ryan. "They must be in *love*!"

"Wait a minute! That's not fair!" I shouted. "So it doesn't matter *what* I say. I'm in love with Andrea whether I want to walk with her or not."

"*Oooooo*, A.J. just admitted he's in love with Andrea!" said Alexia.

"When are you gonna get married?" asked Neil.

If these kids weren't my best friends, I would hate them.

Waiting in Line Stinks

Andrea said she knew where Santa was, and she led us to the other side of the mall. Finally, we found the end of the line of people waiting to meet Santa. There must have been a million hundred kids there! I could see a sign in the distance that said **SANTA'S WORKSHOP**, but Santa Claus was too far away. He was in a special roped-off area.

"We should sneak up to the front of the line," I whispered.

"That would be wrong, Arlo," Andrea said. "These kids got here before we did."

I was going to sneak up anyway, but a big arm came down in front of my face. I looked up. You'll never believe whose arm it was.

Officer Spence, our school security guard! He was standing on a Segway. Those things are cool.

"Officer Spence!" I said. "What are *you* doing here?"

"Making sure everybody waits in line,"

he told me. "And earning a little extra money over the holidays."

"How long will we have to wait in line?" Ryan asked.

"About an hour," Officer Spence said.

"An *hour*?!"

"We could die from old age while we're waiting," I said.

"An hour is like forever,"

said Michael.

Andrea rolled her eyes. "Boys should learn to be patient," she said.

I wasn't sure if it was worth it to wait in line for an hour. I thought that maybe we should just forget about meeting Santa. But that's when I heard these magic words. . . .

"Santa is giving out candy," some kid said.

"Santa is giving out candy,"

said some other kid.

"Santa is giving out candy!" said another kid.

In case you were wondering, everybody was saying that Santa was giving out candy. And if there's one thing that I love almost as much as Santa, it's *candy*. All the candy I got on Halloween was gone.

So we decided to stay in line.

But waiting in lines is boring. To kill the time, I practiced what I was going to say when I got to Santa. . . .

"I want the new Striker Smith Commando action figure with missile launcher, voice activator, attack dog, and deluxe blowtorch. Other accessories sold separately. Batteries not included."

Striker Smith is a superhero from the future who travels through time and fights all who dare to thwart his destiny. He can turn into a jet plane when you push a button on his stomach. His armor suit is tough enough to withstand a nuclear blast. He's a one-man wrecking machine, ready to take on any evil to save the world.

Two Christmases ago, I got my first Striker Smith action figure. Then on the school bus I tied a string to Striker's leg and lowered him out the window so he could fight bad guys who were attacking the bus. But Striker fell under the bus and got decapitated. That's a fancy way of saying his head came off. We had a funeral for his head.*

I got a *new* Striker Smith last Christmas. But he met his untimely end when his head got tragically melted in a battle

* I wrote this poem in his honor: *Ashes to ashes, dust to dusted. / We buried Striker because he was busted. / He was cool, but now he's dead. / It's hard to live without a head.*

with an evil magnifying glass. So now I wanted to get a new Striker, the one that comes with a blowtorch. It is cool.

Most of the other kids in line were little. They didn't even look like they were in first grade yet. Man, I thought, those kids can't even *read*. They don't know what two plus two equals! They don't know *anything*. It's hard to believe that I was that dumb just a few years ago.

Standing still is the most boring thing in the history of the world. What a snoozefest. The line inched forward a little. I could almost see Santa.

"I bet it's not the *real* Santa," I told Alexia. "It's just some guy in a Santa suit."

The little kid in front of me heard that

and turned around. He was holding his mother's hand, and he looked like he was going to cry. He must have been waiting for a long time already. If these kids didn't get to meet Santa soon, they were going to freak out.

A group of grown-ups strolled by the line singing Christmas carols. Somebody else walked by with a real reindeer. There were more reindeer in a petting zoo.

"Where do you think they got those reindeer?" Michael asked me.

"From Rent-A-Reindeer," I told him. "You can rent anything."

Some lady came by asking kids if they wanted to write a letter to Santa and have it delivered to the North Pole. That was a dumb idea. Santa was right here at the mall. Why would I want to send a letter all the way to the North Pole?

"When are we going to get there?" asked Ryan.

"Waiting in line stinks," I said.

"You boys are annoying," Andrea said. "Why don't you go take a walk? Emily and I will hold your place in line."

She didn't have to ask us twice. We got out of there.

A Present for My Sister

"Let's go to Candy Castle!" Ryan shouted as soon as we got out of the line.

"Let's go to Cinnabon," shouted Michael.

"Let's get ice cream!" said Neil the nude kid.

"Let's go to the skateboard shop!" said Alexia.

Malls are cool. There's so much stuff to see and do, especially around Christmastime. Our mall even has a *train* in it.

We ran over to the train. It goes around and around in circles on metal tracks. At the ticket booth was an elf with a funny hat and pointy ears, like on *Star Trek*. The elf turned around, and you'll never believe who it was.

Mrs. Kormel, our bus driver!

"Mrs. Kormel!" I shouted. "What are *you* doing here?"

"Bingle boo!" she said. "I'm running the train . . . and earning a little extra money over the holidays."

"Aren't you a little tall to be an elf?" asked Alexia.

"Elves come in all sizes," Mrs. Kormel told us. "All aboard! *Toot toot!*"

That train ride looked lame, so we didn't get on. Any train that needs an elf to toot for it must be lame.

We ran over to the escalator. Escalators are cooler than trains, and you don't need tickets to ride them. My friend Billy, who lives around the corner, told me that if you run down an up escalator for ten seconds, you'll travel back in time.*

Neil said he had to go to the bathroom, so we went over to the men's room and waited for him to finish. That's when I remembered that my mom gave me money to buy a present for my sister. I didn't know what to get her. What do you get for an annoying sister?

"You're a girl," I said to Alexia. "What do *you* think my sister would like? Perfume? Jewelry?"

---

* That works with revolving doors, too.

47

"Why don't you get her a new skateboard?" suggested Alexia. "That's what I want."

A *skateboard*!

"My sister doesn't even know how to ride a skateboard," I told Alexia. "Why would she want that?"

"No, that's a *great* idea, A.J.!" said Ryan. "Buy your sister a skateboard. Then when she doesn't use it, the skateboard is yours."

"That's *genius*!" I said.

Alexia and Ryan should be in the gifted and talented program.

Neil came out of the bathroom. We were about to go over to the skateboard shop to buy my sister's present when the most amazing thing in the history of the world happened.

It started with a noise—a high-pitched *screech*. At first it was far away. Then it got louder.

And louder.

There was the thunder of feet. They were getting closer.

And closer.

Then there was screaming!

Then we saw a bunch of girls running in our direction. There must have been five hundred of them.

"EEEEEEEEK!" one of them screamed. "I think I see Cray-Z!"

"I love you, Cray-Z!"

Cray-Z was running right at us, and he was being chased by a thundering herd of screaming girls.

"In here!" I yelled to him. "Follow me!"

Ryan, Michael, Neil, and Alexia formed a human wall to stop the girls. I hustled Cray-Z into the men's bathroom. He was gasping for breath. I thought he was gonna die.

He put his hand on my shoulder and looked me in the eye.

"You gotta help me, dude," he said. "Those girls are *nuts*!"

Plenty of Cray-Z to Go Around

The famous Cray-Z was standing right next to me, live and in person!

"I can't take it anymore!" Cray-Z moaned. "They're gonna tear me apart! I need somewhere to hide!"

I didn't know what to say. I didn't know what to do. I had to think fast.

So I did the first thing that came to my mind.

I took off my pants.

"Quick!" I said to Cray-Z. "Let's switch clothes! They'll never know the difference!"

"Good idea!" Cray-Z said, taking off his pants.

I tore off my itchy Christmas sweater and gave it to Cray-Z. He tore off his clothes and gave them to me. I put on his clothes and he put on mine. I looked pretty sharp with his hat and sunglasses. It was hilarious.

"Do I look like you?" I asked him.

"Yeah," he said. "Do I look like *you*?"

"Yeah," I said. "You chill in here for a while. I'll take care of your fans for you."

I pulled the hat down low over my

face, strolled out of the men's room, and gave a big wave to the girls. They started screaming and pulling out cameras to take my picture.

"Look, it's him! It's Cray-Z!"

"I love you!"

"Can I have your autograph?"

Those girls were totally buying it! They really thought I was Cray-Z!

"Sure you can have my autograph," I said.

The girls started sticking pens and paper in my face. I wrote CRAY-Z as fast as my hand could move.

"One at a time, girls," I said cheerfully. "One at a time. There's plenty of Cray-Z to go around."

"EEEEEEK! I touched him!" a little girl screamed. "I'll never wash this hand again!"

After they got my autograph, girls were fainting, crying, and freaking out all over the place. They didn't know that I was just a regular kid. They had no idea that the *real* Cray-Z was hiding in the bathroom.

It was cool to be a famous celebrity. This

was the greatest day of my life!

But you'll never believe who rolled over on his Segway at that moment.

It was Officer Spence, the mall security guard!

Uh-oh. The jig was up. I figured I was in *big* trouble.

"I'm sorry, Mr. Z," said Officer Spence, "but it's time."

"Time for what?" I asked.

"Time for you to sing."

"Huh? What? M-me?" I stammered. "Nobody told me—"

"Hurry up!" Officer Spence said. "They're all waiting for you."

"Who all? Huh? Where?"

Officer Spence grabbed my hand and pulled me up on his Segway. We rolled over to a stage that had been set up near the center of the mall. There were four musicians on the stage wearing Santa hats.

"Get up there!" yelled Officer Spence.

I climbed up on the stage.

"Yo, Z," said the guitar player. "You the *man*."

The girls started screaming. I looked

out at the sea of faces. Some of these fans were younger than me. Some of them were older than me. A few of them looked like my grandma! That was weird. I gave a little wave, and they all started freaking out like they never saw a guy wave before. A guy in a jacket and tie climbed onto the stage and picked up the microphone.

"Okay, boys and girls," he said. "This is the moment you've all been waiting for. Here's the latest pop sensation to sing 'The Christmas Klepto,' his new hit song . . . *Craaaaaaaaaaay-Zeeeee!*"

The girls screamed even louder. The musicians started playing that annoying song. I had no choice. I grabbed the mic and started rapping. . . .

"'Twas the night before Christmas.
You know the rest.
Stuff was all over; the house was all messed.

I was dreaming of a Christmas white.
It was a totally silent night.

That's when I heard a crash and a boom,
So I ran right down to the living room.

There was this guy dressed all in black,
And over his shoulder he carried a sack.

I took one look at him and said, 'Whoa, man!
I know you're not Frosty the Snowman.'

'Who are you?' I asked after a pause.
'You sure don't look like Santa Claus.'

He said, 'The name's Klepto. I'm from the
South Pole.
I grab all your presents. That's how I roll.

'On Christmas Eve I go around the world
and steal all the presents from boys and girls.'"

You know what? Those girls were
digging it! You should have *been* there!
The best part was, they were screaming
so loud that nobody could tell I wasn't the
real Cray-Z. So I kept rapping. . . .

"He went to the corner and got down
on one knee
To scoop up the gifts that were under
our tree.

He took them all. He grabbed my new
toys.
He took my new clothes. He took all
our joy.
To the Christmas Klepto, everything's free.
'I'll take your partridge,' he said, 'and
your pear tree.

'I like your presents, and now they're mine.
Say, how much of this stuff did you buy
online?

'You better watch out. You better not cry.

You make one peep, and I'll poke out

your eye.'

'You're a mean man, sir!' I said with a hiss.

Just wait until Santa finds out about this.'''

I didn't get to finish the song because that guy in the jacket and tie hopped up on the stage again and grabbed the mic away from me.

"Isn't Cray-Z fantastic?" he yelled. "He'll be back at two o'clock to sing for you some more."

The girls screamed. Officer Spence grabbed my hand. I hopped on his

Segway, and he took me back to the men's bathroom.

In the bathroom, Cray-Z was looking in the mirror and combing his hair. When he saw me, he turned around and gave me a hug.

"You saved my life, dude!" he told me. "I owe you one, big-time."

Take a Chill Pill

When I came out of the bathroom wearing my regular clothes, the whole gang clapped me on the back.

"You were *awesome*, A.J.!" said Alexia.

"Those girls didn't suspect a thing," said Ryan.

"How did you know the words to that dumb song?" asked Michael.

"It's been stuck in my head all week!" I admitted.

We hustled through the crowd to get back to Santa's Workshop, all the way at the other end of the mall. It took a long time to find Andrea and Emily. They were close to the front of the line now.

"Where *were* you?" Andrea asked with her mean face on. "What took you so long?"

"It's almost our turn to meet Santa!" said Emily.

"Take a chill pill," I told them. "We're here, right?"

I could see Santa Claus now. He was sitting on this big throne with his red suit, red hat, white beard, and black boots—the whole getup. Santa was fat and jolly, just like I imagined. He was surrounded by Christmas trees, presents, fake snow, and a giant nutcracker on each side.*

"Ho! Ho! Ho!" Santa bellowed.

"Y'know, I'm not sure that's the real Santa," said Neil the nude kid.

"It looks like Santa to me," said Michael.

"I'm so excited!" said Andrea, rubbing her hands together.

Soon it would be our turn. We were on

---

* Man, there must be some big nuts if they need such big nutcrackers.

pins and needles.

Well, not really. We were just standing there. If we were on pins and needles, it would have hurt.

I got up on my tiptoes to look all around. There were so many happy, smiling faces. Christmas trees. Twinkling lights. Jingle bells jingling. It was a beautiful scene.

"Ah," I said, "I love the smell of tinsel at Christmastime."

"Tinsel doesn't smell, dumbhead," said Andrea. "That's pine needles that you smell."

"It's your *face* that I smell," I said.

Why can't a truck full of tinsel fall on Andrea's head?

Just then, one of Santa's elves came running down the line of kids. "It's almost your turn to meet Santa!" she said.

That's when I realized that the elf wasn't a real elf. It was our librarian, Mrs. Roopy! She was dressed up like an elf!

"Mrs. Roopy!" I said. "What are *you* doing here?"

"Who's Mrs. Roopy?" asked Mrs. Roopy. "I'm one of Santa's helpers from the North Pole."

She wasn't fooling anybody. It was Mrs. Roopy for sure. That's when I realized that *all* of Santa's helpers were grown-ups from our school. The guy playing Christmas songs on the organ was our music teacher, Mr. Loring. The lady dressed up like Frosty

the Snowman was our custodian, Miss
Lazar. Another one of the elves was our
Spanish teacher, Miss Holly.

"Miss Holly!" I said when I saw her.
"What are *you* doing here?"

"Earning a little extra money over the holidays," she said. "We all are. *¡Feliz Navidad!*"

"I guess teachers don't get paid very much," said Ryan.

"Teachers get paid?" I asked. "I thought they just came to school every day because they had no place else to go."

There was just one family in front of us in line now. A lady with a big camera came over. I did a double take. The lady was Ms. Hannah, our art teacher!

"Merry Christmas!" she said. "Now listen up. When you sit on Santa's lap, I'm going to snap your picture. So let's see some big smiles, okay?"

"Okay!" we all said.

"Do you want to buy the twenty-dollar package or the forty-dollar package?" Ms. Hannah asked us.

"Package of *what*?" I said.

"Package of pictures, of course," said Ms. Hannah. "The twenty-dollar package includes one eight-by-ten in a nice frame. The forty-dollar package includes *two* framed eight-by-tens and ten wallet-size pictures. I suggest you buy the forty-dollar package so you can share your pictures with your grandparents, your aunts, your uncles. . . ."

What a scam.

"I don't want to buy *any* package," I

told Ms. Hannah.

"Yeah," said Alexia. "We just want to meet Santa."

"Fine," Ms. Hannah said. But she said it in a way that meant "not fine."*

The family in front of us had six annoying kids: three boys and three girls. None of them would sit still. They were all sticking their fingers in Santa's nose, poking him in the eyes, and pulling on his beard. It took like a million hundred hours for Ms. Hannah to take a picture of each of the kids. Then she had to take a picture of just the boys. Then she had to take a picture of just the girls. Then she

---

* Only grown-ups can do that. I guess that's why we go to school—so we can learn how to say one thing and mean the exact opposite thing.

had to take a family picture. I thought I was gonna die from old age.

But finally, the last little whining nerd got up from Santa's lap. It was our turn.

"Okay, which one of you wants to go first?" asked Mrs. Roopy.

"I'm sc-scared of Santa," said Emily, who's scared of everything.

"Me too," said Alexia.

"So am I," said Andrea, Neil, Ryan, and Michael.

I had just sung that dumb rap song in front of a million hundred screaming girls. I wasn't afraid of *anything*.

"I'm not scared," I said. "I'll go first."

This was going to be the greatest moment of my life.

My Turn

I stepped up on the platform where Santa was sitting and climbed on his lap. Ms. Hannah told me to smile, and she snapped my picture.

This was *it*. Everything I had ever done had been leading up to this moment. Now my life was complete. If I suddenly dropped dead, at least I could say that I had met Santa Claus.

That is, if I hadn't dropped dead. Because if you're dead, you can't talk.

"Ho! Ho! Ho!" Santa said as he handed me a candy cane and a coloring book.

Whew! Santa has bad breath!

"Say, little boy, your name isn't A.J. by any chance, is it?"

"How did *you* know?" I asked.

"I'm Santa," Santa said. "I see you when you're sleeping. I know when you're awake."

"That's creepy," I said. "Do you have night vision goggles?"

"Ha! Ha! Ha!" laughed Santa. "No, but I know if you've been bad or good, A.J. Be good for goodness' sake!"

Santa must have a GPS and state-of-the-art surveillance technology. I'm not sure, but I think that's an invasion of privacy.

"So what do you want for Christmas, A.J.?" Santa asked me.

"I want the new Striker Smith

Commando," I said. "It comes with a missile launcher, voice activator, attack dog, and deluxe blowtorch. All other accessories sold separately. Batteries not included."

"Striker Smith?" said Santa. "You mean the superhero action figure from the future who travels through time and fights all who dare to thwart his destiny?"

"Yes!"

Wow, Santa really knows his toys.

"A.J., didn't I bring you a Striker Smith action figure two Christmases ago?" Santa asked me.

"Yeah," I replied. "He fell under the school bus, and his head came off."

"And didn't I bring you *another* Striker

Smith action figure last Christmas?"

"Yeah," I said. "He met his untimely end when his head got tragically melted in a battle with an evil magnifying glass."

"I'm sorry to hear that," Santa said. "I hope you'll take better care of Striker Smith *this* year."

"I will, Santa!"

"Good. Merry Christmas, A.J. Ho! Ho! Ho!"

I looked out at the kids waiting in line. I wondered how Santa would remember which presents we all asked him for.

"Are you going to write down that I asked for a Striker Smith action figure?" I asked Santa.

"That won't be necessary," he replied.

"How will you remember, Santa?"

"My mind is like a steel trap," he told me.

"You catch animals with your head?" I asked.

"No, I mean I have a good memory," Santa told me. "That's how I remember what I bring you each year."

Some of the parents in the crowd were looking at their watches. I guess my time was up. But this might be the only chance in my whole life that I would get to talk with Santa. I didn't want to leave.

"Can I ask you one question, Santa?"

"Sure, A.J."

"I understand how reindeer can fly," I said, "but doesn't your sleigh need a wing on each side, for stability?"

"The Christmas spirit lifts it up," Santa said.

"Yeah, but the sleigh doesn't look very aerodynamic," I told him. "Why not use a helicopter instead?"

"I thought you had just *one* question," Santa said.

"How is it possible to visit every house in the world in one night?" I asked. "What about the houses that don't have chimneys? What about people who live in apartments? How do you fit all the toys in the sleigh? And what do you do the rest of the year?"

"We have to wrap this up, A.J.," said Santa. "There are a lot of children waiting."

"You should really lose some weight," I told him. "Obesity is a big problem these days. Have you checked your cholesterol? Isn't it cold at the North Pole? Is there a supermarket up there? Where do you buy your groceries? Have you considered relocating to a warmer climate? Do the reindeer ever poop on people's heads?"

"Time's up, kid!" one of the parents shouted. "Let's move it along, okay?"

I got up from Santa's lap. But as I was doing that, my itchy Christmas sweater must have got caught on Santa. Because that's when the strangest thing in the history of the world happened.

His beard came off!

The Kid Who Ruined Christmas

"Gasp!" everyone gasped.

"Hey," I said. "You're not the *real* Santa! You're just some guy dressed *up* like Santa!"

"Uh . . . well . . . um . . . ," Santa mumbled.

The fake Santa guy looked really familiar to me. I knew I had seen him somewhere before. So I picked his Santa hat up off his head. And you'll never believe in a million hundred years what was under there.

Nothing!

The guy was completely bald, just like Mr. Klutz, the principal of my school!

In fact, the fake Santa guy *was* Mr. Klutz!

"Mr. Klutz!" I shouted. "What are *you* doing here?"

"Uh . . . earning a little extra money over the holidays," he replied.

I knew I was in trouble as soon as people saw Santa wasn't the real Santa. But I had no idea how much trouble I was in.

"EEEEEEEK!" some girl shouted. "Santa has no hair!"

"He's a fake!" a boy yelled.

"Mommy!" screamed another girl. "You told me that man was the real Santa Claus! You lied!"

All the little kids in line started yelling, screaming, crying, and freaking out. Their parents were upset, too.

"We've been waiting in line for an *hour*," a lady shouted, "and now *this*!"

"It's *that* kid's fault!" one dad yelled,

pointing his finger at me. "He ruined Christmas for my son. He ruined Christmas for *everybody*!"

I thought I was gonna die. Mr. Klutz looked scared. He got up quickly and put a sign on his seat that said **SANTA HAS GONE TO FEED HIS REINDEER. HE'LL BE BACK SOON.**

"I'd better get out of here," he told me.

"A.J., what do you have to say for yourself?"

I didn't know what to say. I didn't know what to do. I had to think fast.

"Uh, peace on earth, goodwill to men?" I said.

"Get him!" somebody shouted. "Get that kid who ruined Christmas!"

Bummer in the winter! There was only one thing I could do.

Run!

The True Meaning of Christmas

This was the worst thing to happen since TV Turnoff Week! I wanted to go to Antarctica and live with the penguins.

I jumped off the little platform to make a run for it, but I slipped on some fake snow and knocked over the Christmas tree. It landed on top of me.

As I was scrambling to get up, my foot

got tangled in a string of Christmas lights. When I yanked at it, sparks started flying.

That must have spooked the reindeer in the petting zoo, because one of them broke out of the gate and started running around in crazy circles.

"Run for your life!" shouted Neil the nude kid. "The reindeer is on the loose!"

"Watch out for those antlers!" a lady screamed.

"It's heading for the food court!" somebody shouted.

I finally got to my feet, and a bunch of angry parents started chasing me.

"Get him!" one of the dads shouted. "Get that kid!"

I bolted out of there. Crowds of people

were all over the place. I had to run around them like a football player to escape the angry parents chasing me. I bumped into some lady, and she fell into a fountain.

"Help!" I shouted. "They're gonna kill me!"

I ran up the down escalator. Then I ran down the up escalator. But I didn't travel through time. The parents were still chasing me. I couldn't lose them!

At the other end of the mall, I spotted the men's bathroom. Maybe I could hide in a stall, I figured. It was my only hope.

I ran over there and ducked inside the bathroom. I was panting and gasping for breath.

And you'll never believe who was in

there, combing his hair in the mirror.

Cray-Z!

"Dude!" he said. "What's the matter? You look like you've been through a war!"

I put my hand on his shoulder and looked him in the eye.

"You've got to help me!" I begged. "I was sitting on Santa's lap, and I accidentally pulled off his beard. The kids who were waiting in line freaked out, and now their parents are trying to get me! What should I do?"

"Quick!" Cray-Z said. "Let's switch clothes again!"

"Huh?"

"Just do it!"

I tore off my itchy Christmas sweater

and gave it to Cray-Z. He tore off his clothes and gave them to me.

"Now get out of here!" Cray-Z said. "And act casual."

I whistled as I strolled out of the bathroom.* A bunch of angry parents were milling around, looking all over. None of them noticed me. I thought I was in the clear.

But that's when the most amazing thing in the history of the world happened. An announcement came over the public address system.

Well, that's not the amazing part, because announcements come over the

---

* Because if you're whistling, nobody thinks you did anything wrong. That's the first rule of being a kid.

public address system all the time. The amazing part was what happened next.

"Attention, shoppers. It's two o'clock. The young pop sensation Cray-Z is about to do some more Christmas rapping on the main stage near the big tree. Come see him perform!"

Suddenly, Officer Spence came rolling over to me on his Segway.

"We've been looking all over for you, Mr. Z!" he said. "Come on! Everybody's waiting!"

"Huh? What? Who? Me? Again?" I asked.

Officer Spence pulled me up on the Segway and rolled over to the stage.

"Yo, Z," said the guitar player. "Let's rock, man."

There must have been a million hundred girls in the audience now. Some of them were trying to climb up on the stage, but the police were holding them back. That guy in the jacket and tie climbed up and took the microphone.

"Okay, boys and girls," he said. "Here he is again. The latest. The greatest . . . *Craaaaaaaaaaaay-Zeeeee!*"

The girls started screaming. The band started playing. I had no choice. So I started rapping. . . .

"'Twas the night before Christmas.
You know the rest.
Stuff was all over; the house was all messed.

I was dreaming of a Christmas white.
It was a totally silent night.

That's when I heard a crash and a boom,
So I ran right down to the living room.

There was this guy dressed all in black,
And over his shoulder he carried a sack.

I took one look at him and said, 'Whoa, man!
I know you're not Frosty the Snowman.'

'Who are you?' I asked after a pause.
'You sure don't look like Santa Claus.'

He said, 'The name's Klepto. I'm from
the South Pole.

I grab all your presents. That's how I roll.

'On Christmas Eve I go around the world
and steal all the presents from boys and girls.'

He went to the corner and got down on
one knee
To scoop up the gifts that were under
our tree.

He took them all. He grabbed my new toys.
He took my new clothes. He took all
our joy.

To the Christmas Klepto, everything's free.
'I'll take your partridge,' he said, 'and
your pear tree.

'I like your presents, and now they're mine.
Say, how much of this stuff did you buy online?

'You better watch out. You better not cry.
You make one peep, and I'll poke out your eye.'

'You're a mean man, sir!' I said with a hiss.
Just wait until Santa finds out about this.'

That Mr. Klepto thought he was a smarty,
But in the end, we spoiled his party.

Oh sure, the guy had lots of charm,
Until he tripped our silent alarm.

A few minutes later, the cops arrived.
Mr. Klepto, under the couch he dived.

The cops yelled, 'Come out with your
hands in the air.'
'I was framed!' he shouted. 'This ain't
fair!'

The cops said, 'Now don't try anything
violent.
All you have is the right to remain silent.'

They dragged him away, and he said,
'Bye-bye.'
And that was the last I heard of that
guy.

Now all this stuff that I've been rappin'
You may say that none of it happened.

After all, nobody came and stole your stuff.
Nobody broke in. Nobody got rough.

Well, the reason that you've got nothing to fear
Is because they put Klepto away for ten years!

So you can believe what you want to believe,
But that's what happened on Christmas Eve."

"Let's hear it for Cray-Z!" said the guy with the jacket and tie.

The girls went nuts, screaming and yelling and freaking out. I jumped off the stage and ran back to the men's room. Cray-Z was in there waiting for me.

"You saved my life," I told him.

"Now we're even, dude."

Cray-Z and I switched back into our normal clothes, shook hands, and said good-bye. As I was about to walk away, I came up with the greatest idea in the history of the world.

"Hey, Cray-Z. I need to get a Christmas present for my sister. Can you give me an autograph?"

"Sure, dude," he said.

Cray-Z took off his hat. He pulled a Sharpie from his pocket, signed the hat, and handed it to me.

"Y'know," he said, "sometimes I wish I was in your shoes."

"Why?" I asked. "What's wrong with *your* shoes?"

"No," he said, "what I mean is that the grass is always greener on the other side."

"Huh?" I asked. "What does the color of grass have to do with anything?"

That Cray-Z kid is weird. Who cares about shoes and grass?

But as I walked away, I started thinking about what Cray-Z said. Christmas isn't about malls and elves and trees and presents. It's about being a good person. It's about helping a guy out when he's in trouble. Cray-Z needed my help, so I helped him. Then I needed *his* help, and he helped me. Christmas is a time for giving. *That's* the true meaning of Christmas spirit.

Who knows? Maybe I'll become Cray-Z's stunt double. Maybe Santa will bring me the new Striker Smith Commando action figure with missile launcher, voice activator, attack dog, and deluxe blowtorch. Maybe another song will get stuck in my head. Maybe the real Santa will come to the mall next Christmas.

Maybe they'll pay the teachers more money so they don't have to dress up like elves. Maybe I'll travel back in time on an escalator. Maybe Santa will get some breath mints. Maybe I won't have to wear my itchy Christmas sweater next year. Maybe I'll get to eat some of those giant nuts. Maybe Santa will be arrested for invading people's privacy. Maybe Mr. Klutz will catch animals with his head. Maybe Santa will ditch his sleigh and switch to a helicopter. Maybe Andrea and Emily will bring peace and harmony to kids all over the world.

But it won't be easy!

Deck the Halls, We're Off the Walls!

Weird Extras!

★ Professor A.J.'s Weird Christmas Facts

★ Fun Games and Weird-Word Puzzles

★ My Weird School Trivia Questions

PROFESSOR A. J.'S WEIRD CHRISTMAS FACTS

Howdy, My Weird School fans! Professor
A.J. here. I'm gonna tell you a bunch of
stuff you probably don't know about
Christmas. It's really important for you
to learn stuff so you won't grow up to be
a dumbhead like a certain person in my
class with curly brown hair who rolls her
eyes and says mean things to me all the
time. But it wouldn't be polite to name
names.*

First of all, do you know how the tradition
of the Christmas tree got started? It was

---

* Andrea

back in 1897. On Christmas Eve that year, a huge pine tree fell on top of a house in Lake Placid, New York. The Bates family was just sitting down to their Christmas dinner when the tree crashed through their roof and landed in their living room. The family freaked out and were really angry that they would have to spend their Christmas Eve getting that dumb tree out of their living room. So they decided just to leave it there. And ever since that day, people have been putting trees in their living rooms at Christmastime.

Okay, I totally made that story up, so nah-nah-nah boo-boo on you!

But here's some *true* stuff about Christmas. . . .

—The first song to be broadcast from space was "Jingle Bells", on December 16, 1965. The crew of the *Gemini 6* sang the song and played a harmonica.

Most people don't know that the astronauts *wanted* to play the song on a piano, but it wouldn't fit in the space capsule.

JINGLE BELLS...
JINGLE BELLS...

FACT:
—Do you know what the word "mistletoe" really means? You better sit down for this one. Mistletoe means "dung on a twig."

That's right! Bird dung! Honest, I did not make that up. You can't make up stuff that good.

FACT:

—You know that character Tiny Tim in Charles Dickens's classic *A Christmas Carol*? Well, before he named the character Tiny Tim, Dickens considered naming the character Puny Pete, Small Sam, or Little Larry.

Ha! I bet that book would have sold a lot more copies if he titled it *Puny Pete Has Nothing to Eat!*

FACT:

—The coolest shopping mall in the world is the **Mall of the Emirates** in **Dubai**. Do you know why? Because it has its own indoor ski slope!

Can you believe that? Dubai is in the desert, so they put in a ski slope. That's weird.

FACT:

—In Columbus, Texas, they have a Santa Claus Museum. There are more than two thousand Santas on display.

The museum even has a Santa doorbell!

FACT:

—Foreign languages are weird. If you wanted to say "Merry Christmas" in Italian, you'd say "*Buon Natale.*" In Spanish it's "*Feliz Navidad.*" In French it's "*Joyeux Noël.*" In German it's "*Frohe Weihnachten.*"

And if you were in outer space and you said "Merry Christmas" to somebody, you would die instantly, because there's no oxygen in outer space.

FACT:

—In Italy they celebrate Christmas on January 6. They call it the Feast of the Epiphany. A witch called La Befana rides on her broomstick the night before and fills kids' stockings with presents if they're good and lumps of coal if they're bad.

That's why I'll never go to Italy over Christmas vacation. First of all, boys have to wear stockings. Not only that, but you might have to walk around in stockings with coal in them. That would hurt!

FACT:

—**Speaking of stockings, kids once used their regular old socks for presents from Santa. That came from an old Dutch tradition in which kids would leave their shoes out with food for Saint Nicholas's donkeys, and he would leave presents in return.**

Ugh, disgusting! Dutch people put food in their shoes and let donkeys eat out of them. They're weird.

FACT:
—Did you know that the United States has an official Christmas tree? It's a giant sequoia in California that's over 1,500 years old.

Wow, that's almost as old as my parents.

I could tell you a lot more stuff about Christmas, but I'd rather open my presents and go play out in the snow. Happy holidays!

Professor A.J. (the professor of awesomeness)

FUN GAMES AND WEIRD-WORD PUZZLES

I. WHERE'S SANTA?

Directions: Santa needs to deliver his gifts, but he doesn't want to be seen! Can you find where he is hidden in this picture?

2. WINTER WORD JUMBLE

Directions: The eight words below are all jumbled up! Can you put the letters in correct order and uncover the holiday words?

1. PNSRETE: _____

2. YJO: _____

3. WOSMNAN: _____

4. SBLLE: _____

5. EGIHLS: _____

6. SCHNETTSU: _____

7. CNRAUERTKC: _____

8. DRNEIREE: _____

3. GIFT GIVER

Directions: Everyone has something special they want for Christmas. Match these weird people and animals below with the gift that they would most want from Santa!

4. SNOWFLAKE MATCH

Directions: Snowflakes are falling! Each snowflake is an identical match with another snowflake on the page. Can you find all the matches?

5. CRAZY-CHRISTMAS WORD SEARCH

Directions: Can you find all ten Christmas words that are hidden in this messy jumble of letters?

```
E K A L F W O N S E F U V S M
M O E Z V L X Q I V L D X I W
Q X C L H X D Y W L D F S K M
U M A F O Q S X W F O T X I P
C D N G H P E W J F L W T H X
R W D K C L H K X E D A P T I
K Y Y I X H Z T T M R K A S U
B C C A X J R O R E D C G T X
X V A H J F E I T O G G C N R
B L N B H X B N S W N B I E Y
B C E N T U I W Q T H N S S G
I F Q Y H W O F J L M R B E M
J I N G L E B E L L S A M R V
A N G E L D W W P Q M W S P A
Y S U N Z M F I P S R X K A P
```

**ANGEL CHRISTMAS ELF JINGLE BELLS
MISTLETOE CANDY CANE NORTH POLE
PRESENTS SNOWFLAKE WINTER**

6. ORNAMENT OOPS

Directions: The ornaments on this Christmas tree all spell special holiday words, but it seems that a few have gone missing! Can you figure out the missing letters in each of these words? After you've found all of the letters, put them in order on the lines below the tree to reveal the answer to the mystery question!

Who Is Santa's Favorite Helper?

__ __ __. __ __ __ __ __

MY WEIRD SCHOOL
TRIVIA QUESTIONS

There's no way in a million hundred years you'll get all these answers right. So nah-nah-nah boo-boo on you!

Q: WHAT IS A.J.'S SISTER'S NAME?
A: Amy

Q: WHICH STAFF MEMBER INVENTED A SECRET LANGUAGE THAT MAKES NO SENSE?
A: Mrs. Kormel

Q: WHAT IS MS. HANNAH'S DRESS MADE OF?
A: Pot holders she bought on eBay

Q: WHERE DO THE KIDS EAT LUNCH?
A: In the vomitorium

Q: HOW DID MISS SMALL BREAK HER LEG?
A: She fell out of a tree.

Q: WHAT DOES ANDREA DO EVERY THURSDAY AFTER SCHOOL?
A: Clog dancing

Q: WHAT IS ANDREA'S FAVORITE MOVIE?
A: Annie

Q: WHO DOES A.J. WANT TO MARRY WHEN HE GROWS UP?
A: Mrs. Cooney, the nurse

Q: WHAT DOES YAWYE STAND FOR?
A: You Are What You Eat

Q: WHO IS ELLA MENTRY SCHOOL NAMED AFTER?
A: Ella Mentry

Q: WHAT DOES MISS LAZAR HAVE IN HER SECRET ROOM DOWN IN THE BASEMENT?
A: A museum of toilet-bowl plungers

Q: WHY DOESN'T A.J. HAVE AN INVISIBLE FRIEND ANYMORE?
A: He got into an argument with his invisible friend, so they stopped being friends.

Q: WHAT FUEL POWERS MR. DOCKER'S CAR?
A: Potatoes

Q: WHAT IS BRAINWASHING?
A: That's when bald guys shampoo their head

Q: WHAT IS A.J.'S FAVORITE HOLIDAY?
A: Take Our Daughters to Work Day, because Andrea is absent from school

Q: WHY IS PRESIDENT'S DAY SPECIAL, ACCORDING TO MICHAEL?
A: Because that's the day big-screen TVs go on sale

Q: WHY ARE SHOVELS BETTER THAN COMPUTERS?
A: Because you can't dig a hole with a computer

Q: WHAT DOES IT MEAN WHEN TEACHERS MAKE A PEACE SIGN WITH THEIR FINGERS?
A: It means "shut up."

Q: WHY DO YOU CLAP AT THE END OF AN ASSEMBLY?
A: Because you're glad it's over.

Q: HOW DOES MRS. YONKERS POWER HER COMPUTER?
A: She runs on a giant hamster wheel.

Q: WHAT IS SPECIAL ABOUT MRS. YONKERS'S PENCIL SHARPENER?
A: It is remote-controlled.

Q: WHAT IS DR. CARBLES'S FIRST NAME?

A: He wants to be Frank, but his name is Milton.

Q: WHERE DOES MR. KLUTZ GET A PIG?

A: From Rent-A-Pig.

ANSWER KEY

WHERE'S SANTA?

!

WINTER WORD JUMBLE

1. PNSRETE: PRESENT
2. YJO: JOY
3. WOSMNAN: SNOWMAN
4. SBLLE: BELLS
5. EGIHLS: SLEIGH
6. SCHNETTSU: CHESTNUTS
7. CNRAUERTKC: NUTCRACKER
8. DRNEIREE: REINDEER

GIFT GIVER

SNOWFLAKE MATCH

CRAZY-CHRISTMAS
WORD SEARCH

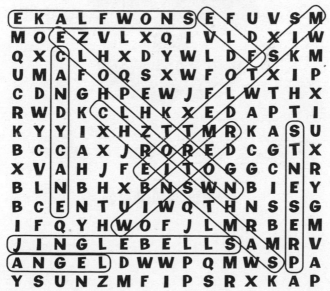

ORNAMENT OOPS

WHO IS SANTA'S FAVORITE HELPER?

MRS. CLAUS